ISSUE # 1

O.T.A.B.I.S
OMNI.TOOL.AUGMENTED.BIOTECH.INTERSTELLAR.SUIT

"ACCIDENTAL DESTINY"

CREATED BY
DEION TILLETT

To order additional copies of this book, contact:
Xlibris
844-714-8691
www.Xlibris.com
Orders@Xlibris.com

ISBN: Softcover   978-1-6641-9644-5
       EBook   978-1-6641-9643-8

Print information available on the last page

Rev. date: 10/22/2021

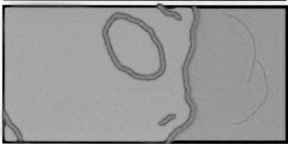

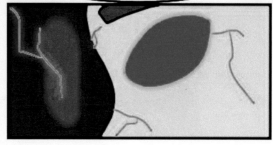

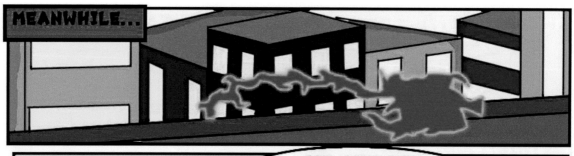

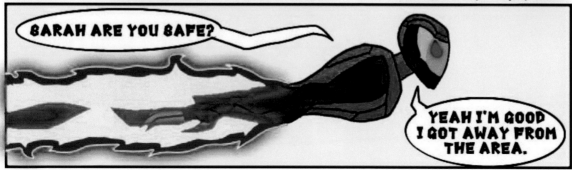

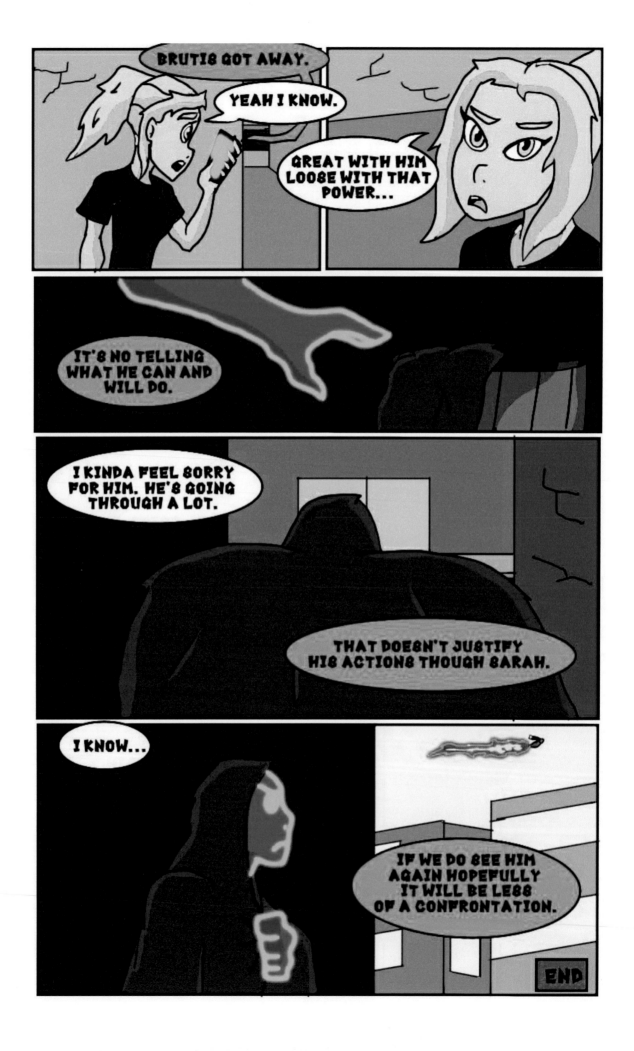

Printed in the United States
by Baker & Taylor Publisher Services